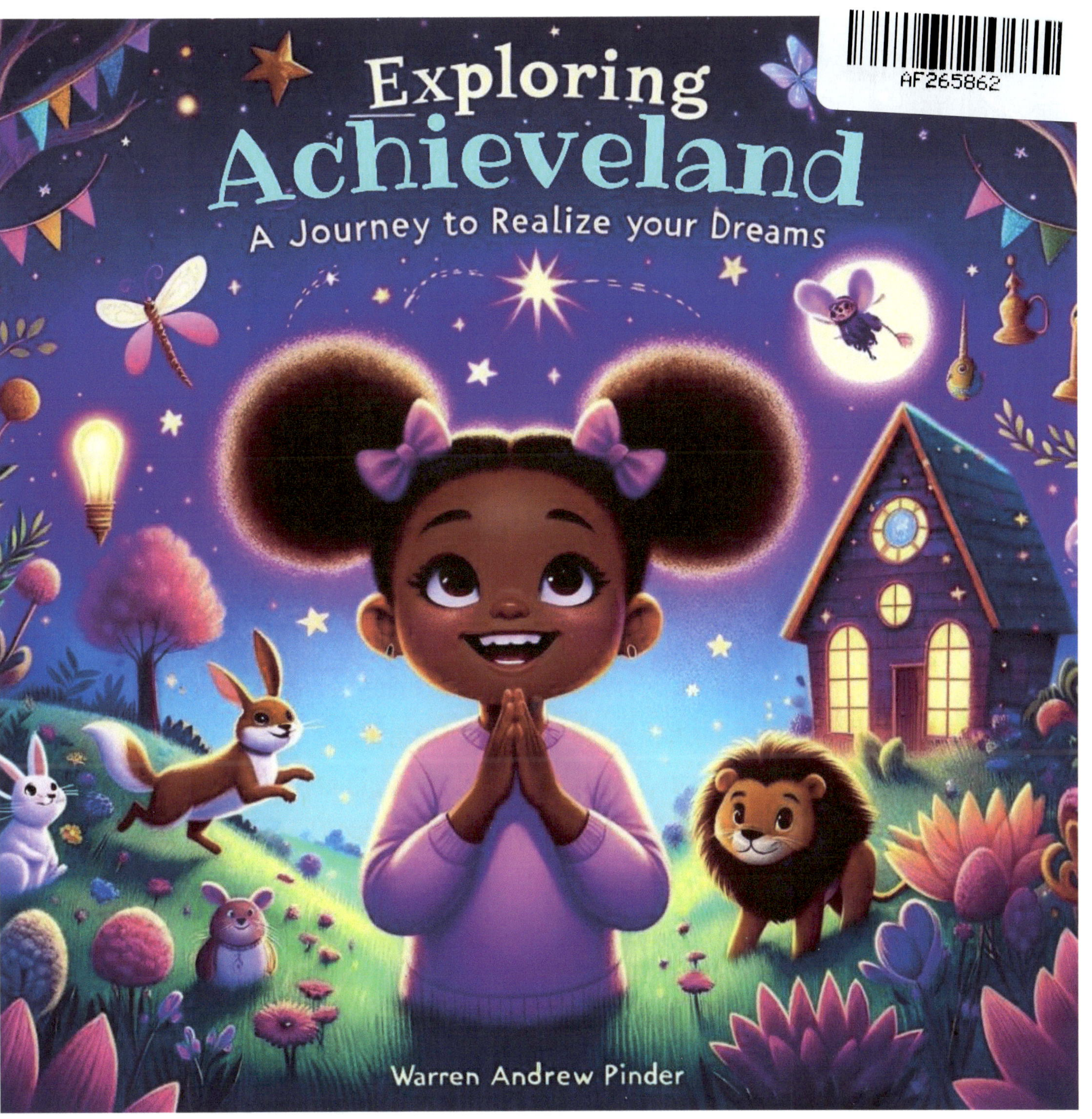

Exploring Achieveland
A Journey to Realize your Dreams
Warren Andrew Pinder

Author: Warren Andrew Pinder
Published by: Achieve-Movement Inc.
Book Design & Illustration by: Dr. Naqib Khan
ISBN # 978-1-0688290-0-0 (Paperback)
ISBN # 978-1-0688290-1-7 (Kindle)
Printed in Canada

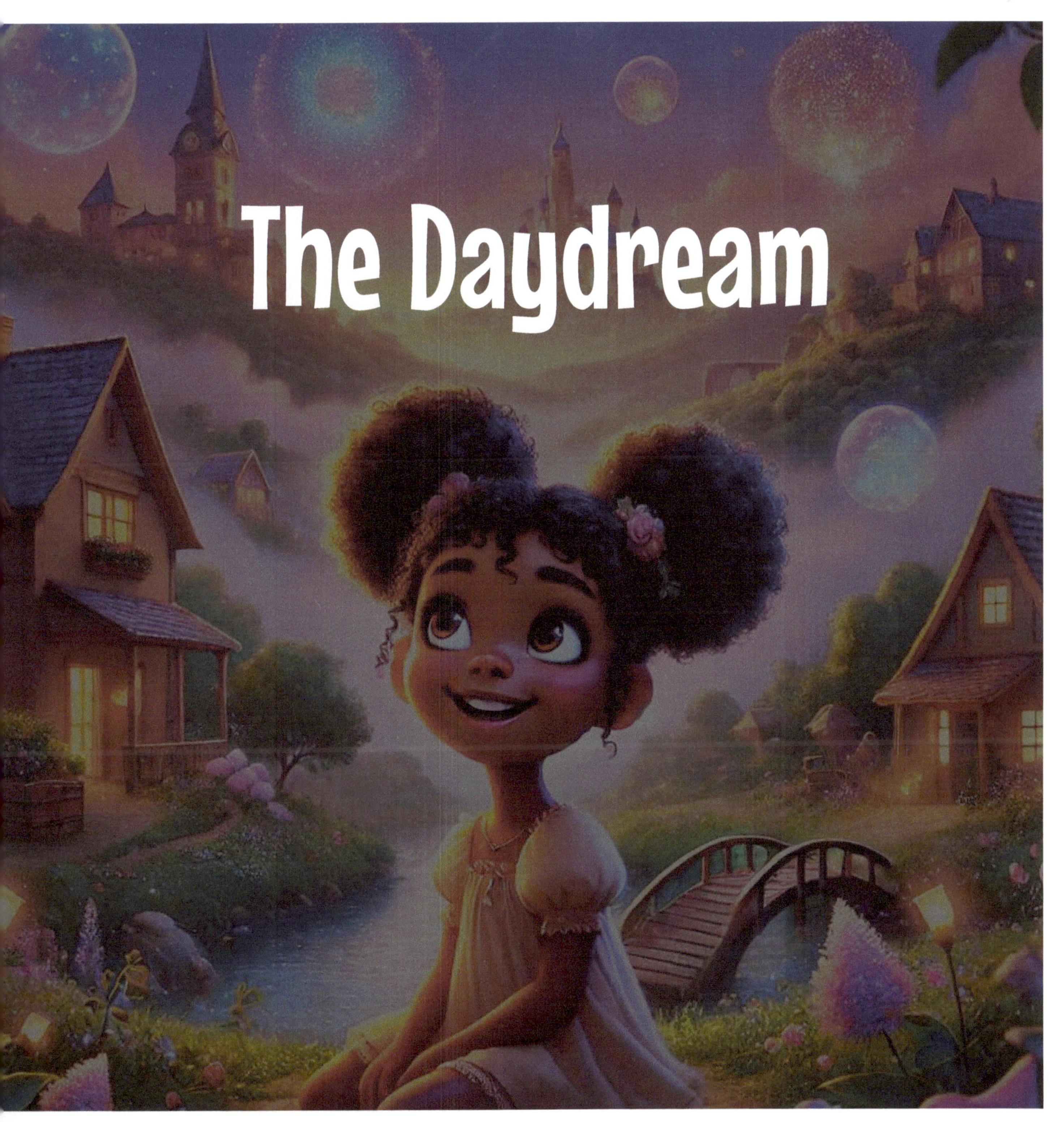
The Daydream

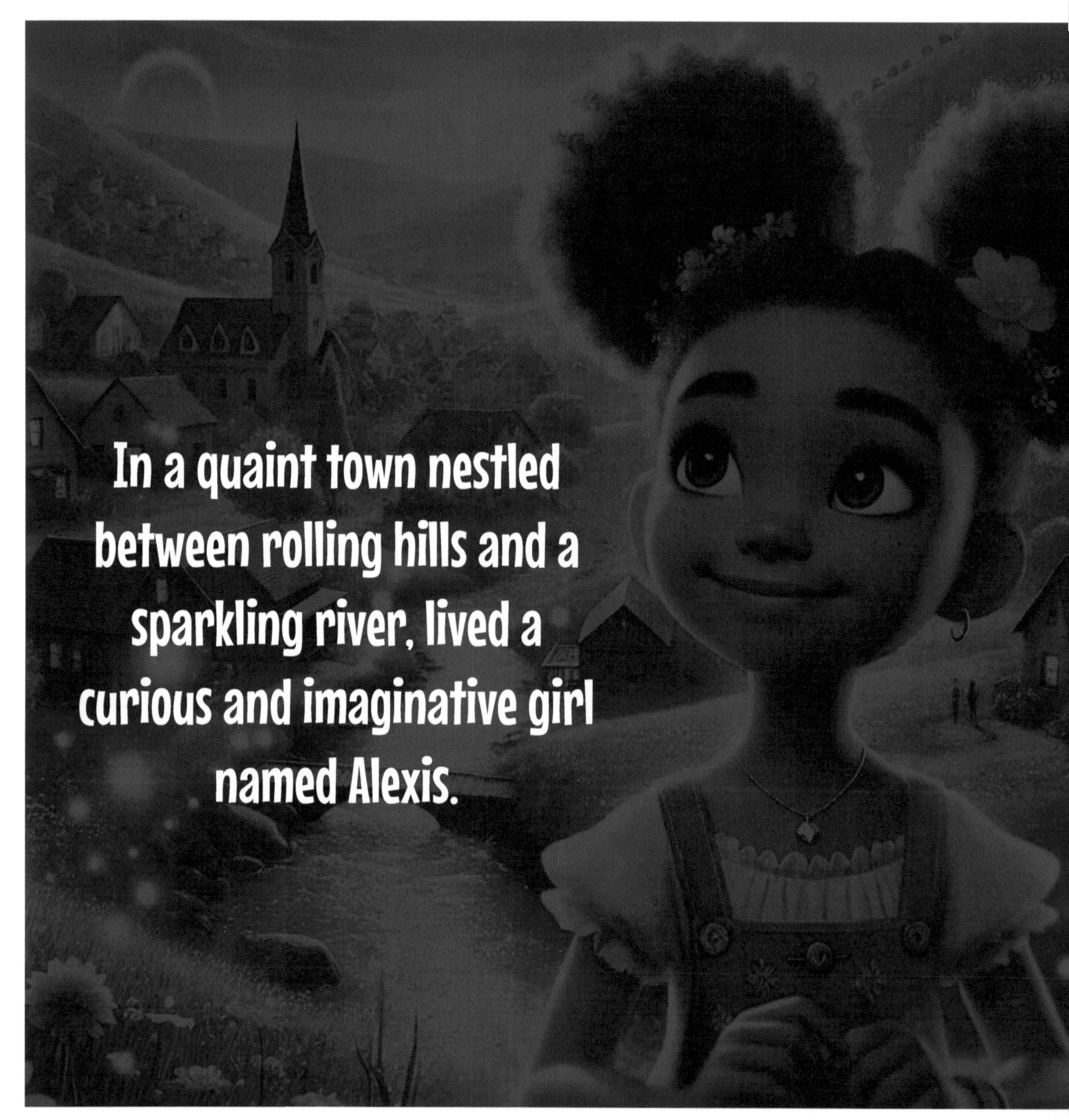

In a quaint town nestled
between rolling hills and a
sparkling river, lived a
curious and imaginative girl
named Alexis.

She was known for her special talent: daydreaming. Whenever her mind wandered, it would always lead to a magical place known as "Achieve-land."

One bright and sunny afternoon, while
sitting under a large oak tree in the park,
watching the fluffy white clouds drift by,
Alexis' mind began to wander once again.

This time, the daydream was different. It felt like a gentle breeze lifting her off the ground and carrying her to a place she had only imagined before.

To her amazement, when Alexis opened her eyes, she found herself standing in the heart of Achieve-land.

Meeting
The Achievians

In Achieve-land, the sky was painted with a breathtaking shade of purple, and the grass twinkled like a thousand stars.

As Alexis explored this enchanting world, she encountered a group of extraordinary creatures known as the "Achievians." Each Achievian had a fascinating tale to tell:

Sparkle
The Sparkling Firefly

Sparkle was a firefly with an idea
so bright it lit up the night. She
used to hide in the shadows,
fearing her own light.

But one starry night, she realized that her glow could conquer the darkness. She shared her story under a sky filled with a myriad of stars, inspiring Alexis to shine her own light.

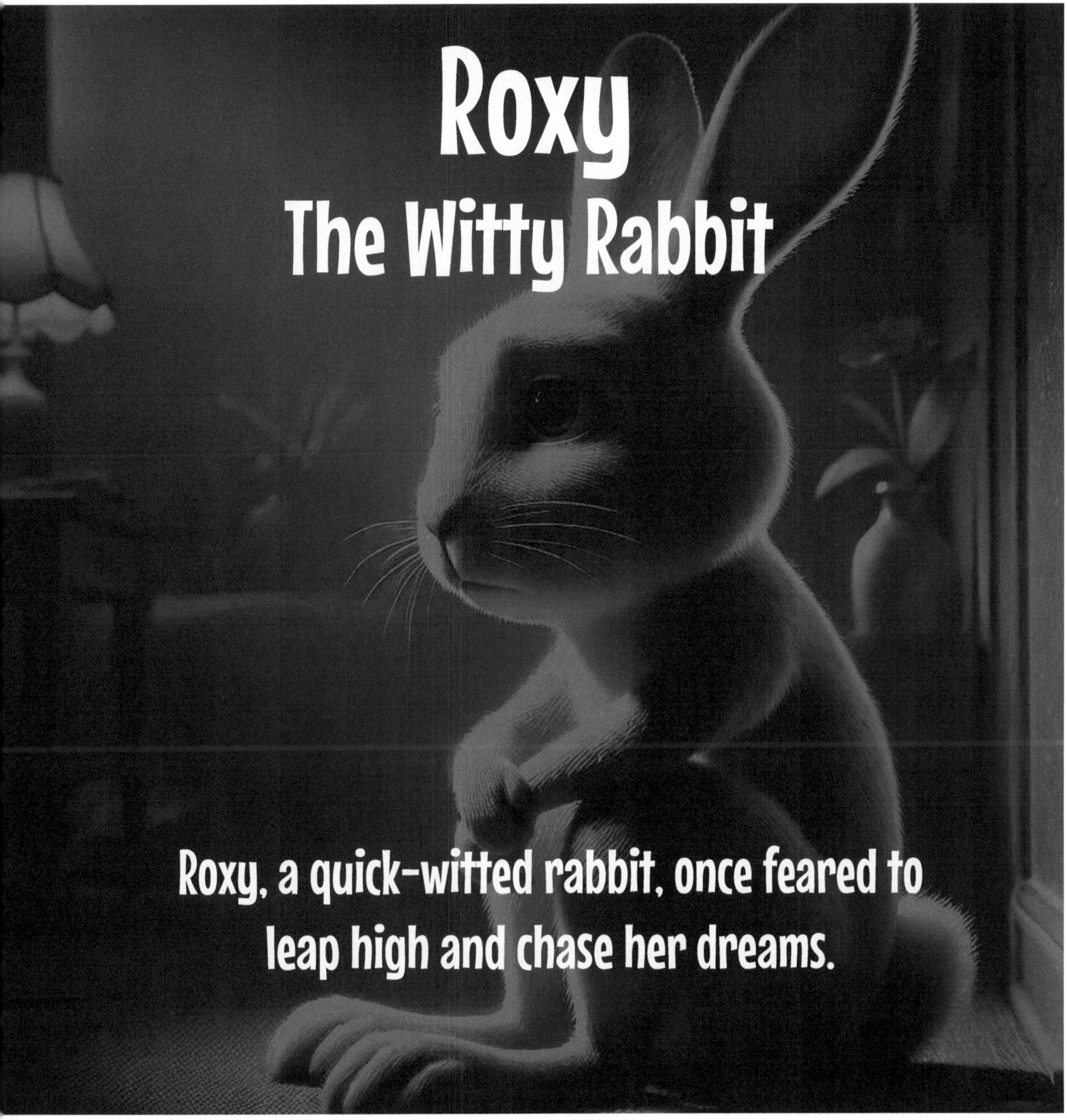

Roxy
The Witty Rabbit

Roxy, a quick-witted rabbit, once feared to leap high and chase her dreams.

She overcame her hesitation by bounding over a series of hurdles and achieving victory in a race of determination. Her story stirred Alexis' own courage.

Leo
The Lion Who Roars

Leo was a lion with a mighty roar, but he once doubted his own power.

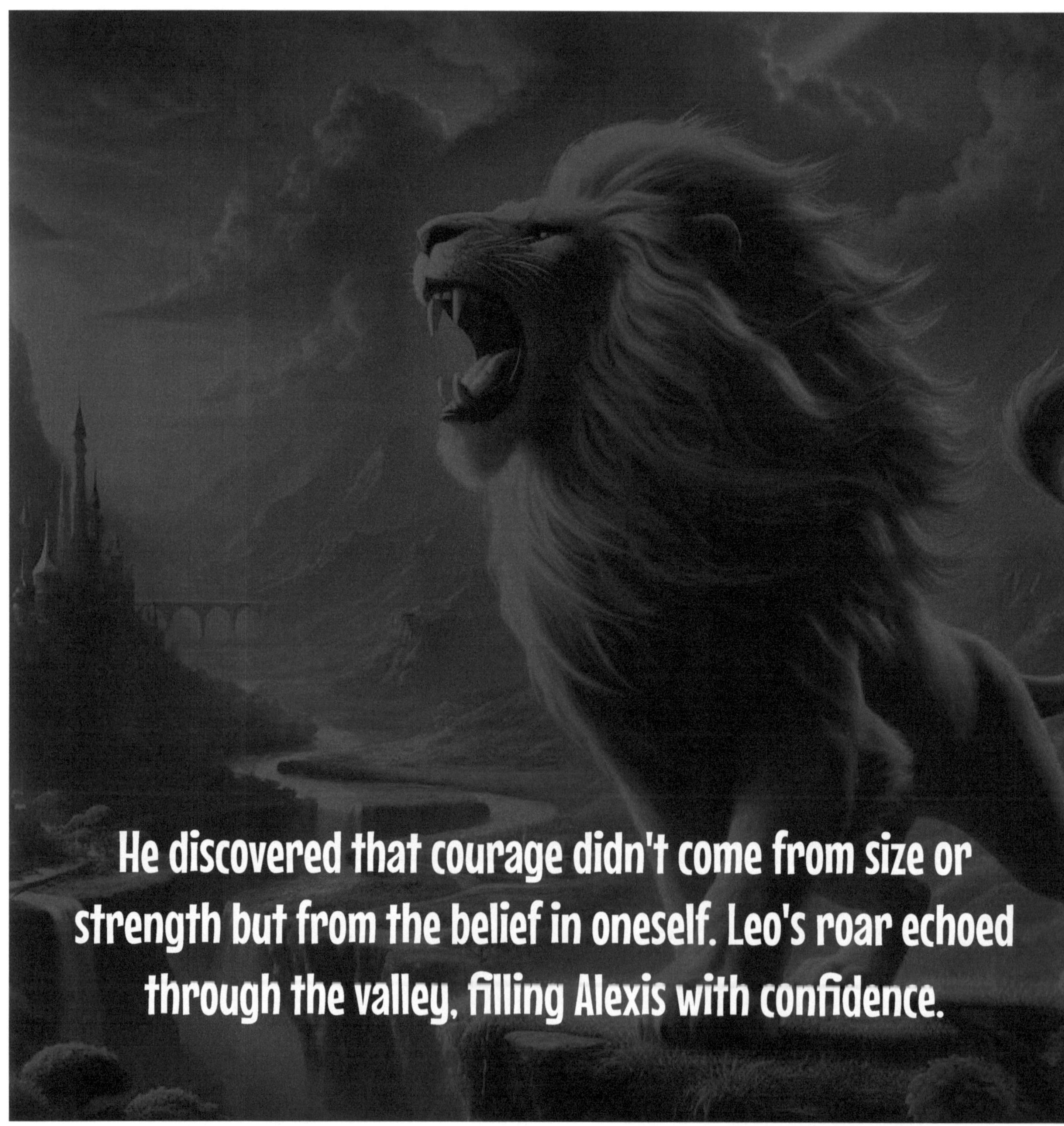

He discovered that courage didn't come from size or strength but from the belief in oneself. Leo's roar echoed through the valley, filling Alexis with confidence.

Luna
The Wise

Luna, the owl, had always been wise beyond her years, yet she once doubted her ability to lead and inspire.

She conquered her shyness and embraced her wisdom to become the guide and mentor of Achieve-land. Alexis, listening to her tales of transformation, found a mentor in Luna.

Ziggy
The Quick Thinker

Ziggy, a quick-thinking squirrel, had a knack for solving puzzles. He once faced a mind-bending maze with ever-changing paths.

Ziggy's cleverness eventually led him to the exit.
Alexis, fascinated by his tale, understood the
importance of creativity and persistence.

Bella
The Beautiful

Bella, a butterfly, once struggled with impatience as she awaited her transformation.

She learned to appreciate her own journey,
understanding that true beauty comes with time.
Alexis, watching Bella flutter gracefully among the
flowers, grasped the value of patience.

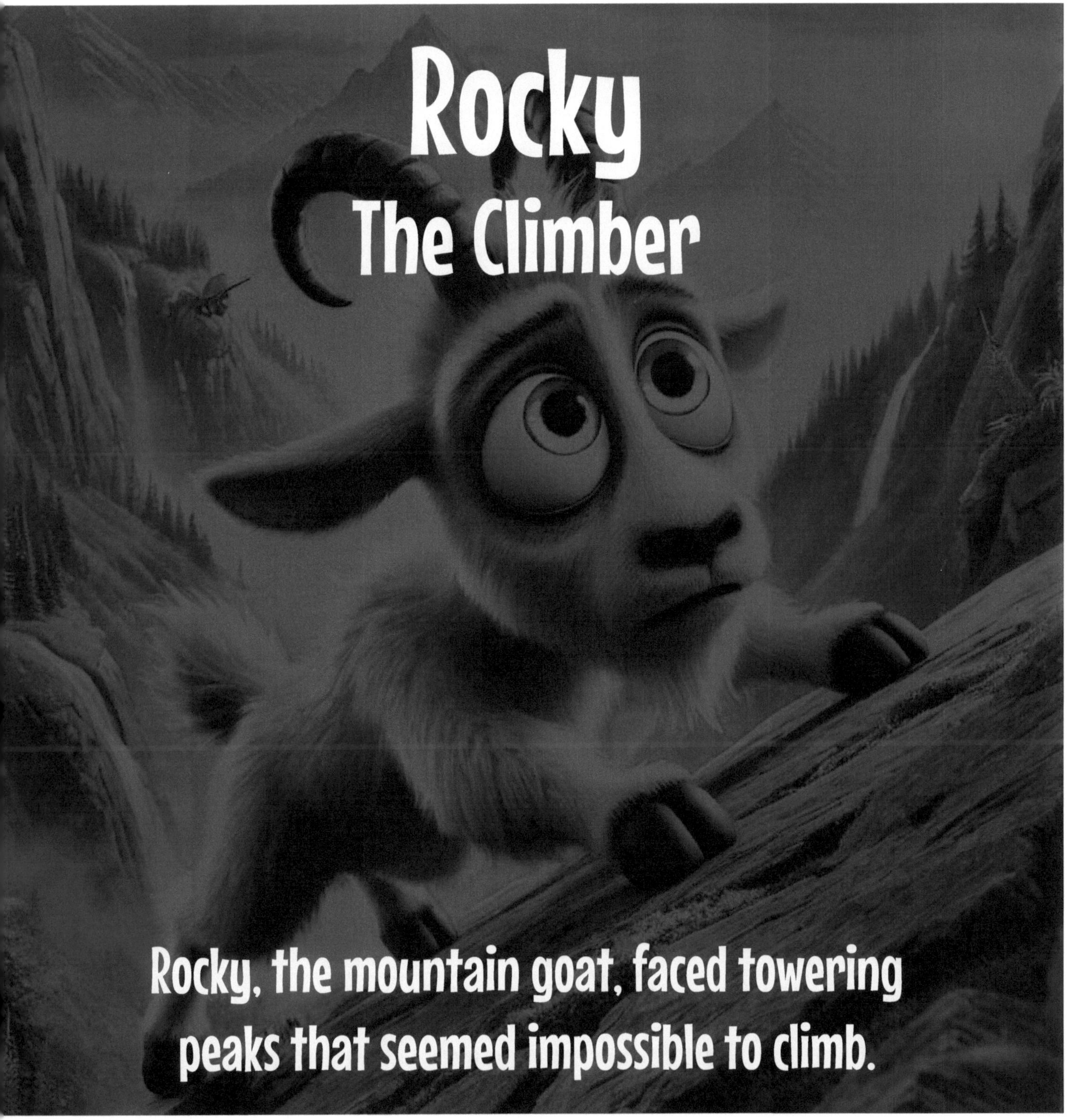

Rocky
The Climber

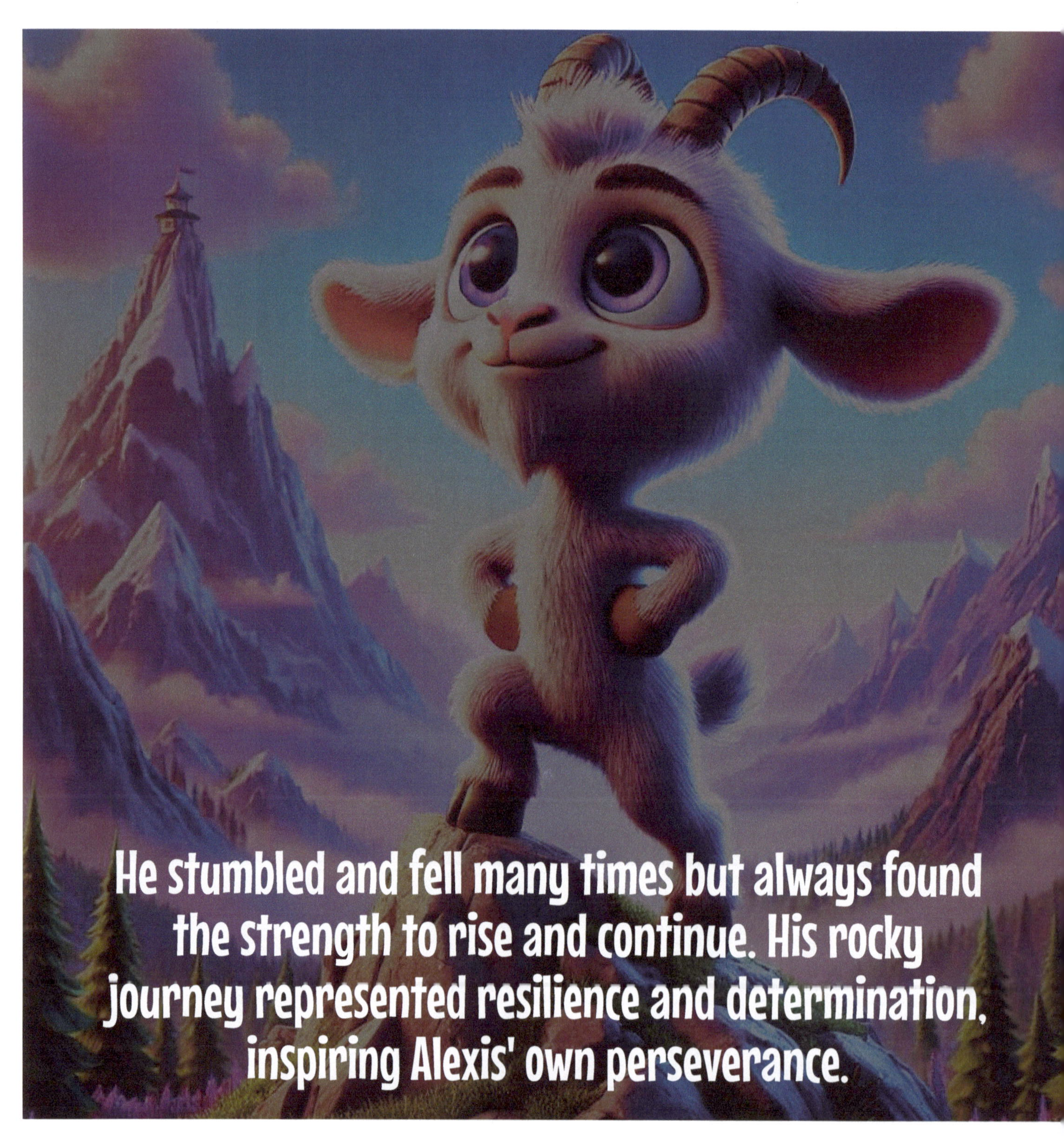
He stumbled and fell many times but always found the strength to rise and continue. His rocky journey represented resilience and determination, inspiring Alexis' own perseverance.

These remarkable Achievians became more than friends; they became mentors and muses, each with a unique story that ignited a spark of determination within Alexis.

As Alexis continued her journey through Achieve-land, she encountered special challenges that matched the stories of the Achievians:

One day, Alexis came across a twisting maze made of mirrors. At first, she felt hesitant, doubting herself just like the twists and turns of the maze. But she took a deep breath and chose to believe in herself. She realized that self-belief is like a light that can break through the biggest doubts.

Another time, Alexis reached a rushing river with a bridge that swayed with each step. It seemed so scary, but she remembered Roxy's story of bravery. With each step she took, she felt her courage grow stronger. She learned that courage means taking a deep breath and taking a step forward even when you're scared.

In a dense forest filled with confusing paths, Alexis
felt lost. She didn't know which way to go. Luna, Ziggy,
Bella, and Rocky joined her and taught her that just
like a puzzle, the forest had a solution.

Luna's wisdom was like a map, Ziggy's clever thinking was like solving a puzzle, Bella's patience helped her stay calm, and Rocky's strength was like a reassuring hand on her shoulder. She learned that even in uncertainty, there's always a way to find your path.

These challenges weren't just obstacles; they were life lessons for Alexis. They showed her that believing in herself, being brave, and staying calm in uncertain times were the keys to unlocking her true potential.

At the heart of Achieve-land, Alexis met the wisest character of all, the "Dream Weaver." This mystical figure lived in a grand treehouse with windows that sparkled like diamonds. The Dream Weaver had a gentle smile and eyes filled with endless wisdom.

With the Dream Weaver's guidance, Alexis discovered her deepest dream: to become a marine biologist and explore the mysteries of the ocean. Together, they created a plan to reach this dream and planted a flag in Achieve-land to symbolize their commitment.

As the sun began to set in Achieve-land, Alexis knew it was time to leave and return to the real world. With newfound confidence and a determination to bring the Achieve-land mindset with her, Alexis bid farewell to her new friends, the Achievians.

Back in the real world, Alexis shared her extraordinary adventure with friends and family. She discovered that Achieve-land wasn't a place that existed only in her dreams; it was a mindset and a source of inspiration that lived within her.

Together, they set goals, worked hard, and supported each other in their pursuit of dreams. They learned that with a positive attitude, determination, and belief in themselves, they could turn any dream into a reality.

And so, Achieve-land became a place not just in Alexis' dreams but in her heart. It was a place where the magic of believing in herself was always within reach, waiting to inspire and guide her on her journey to success.

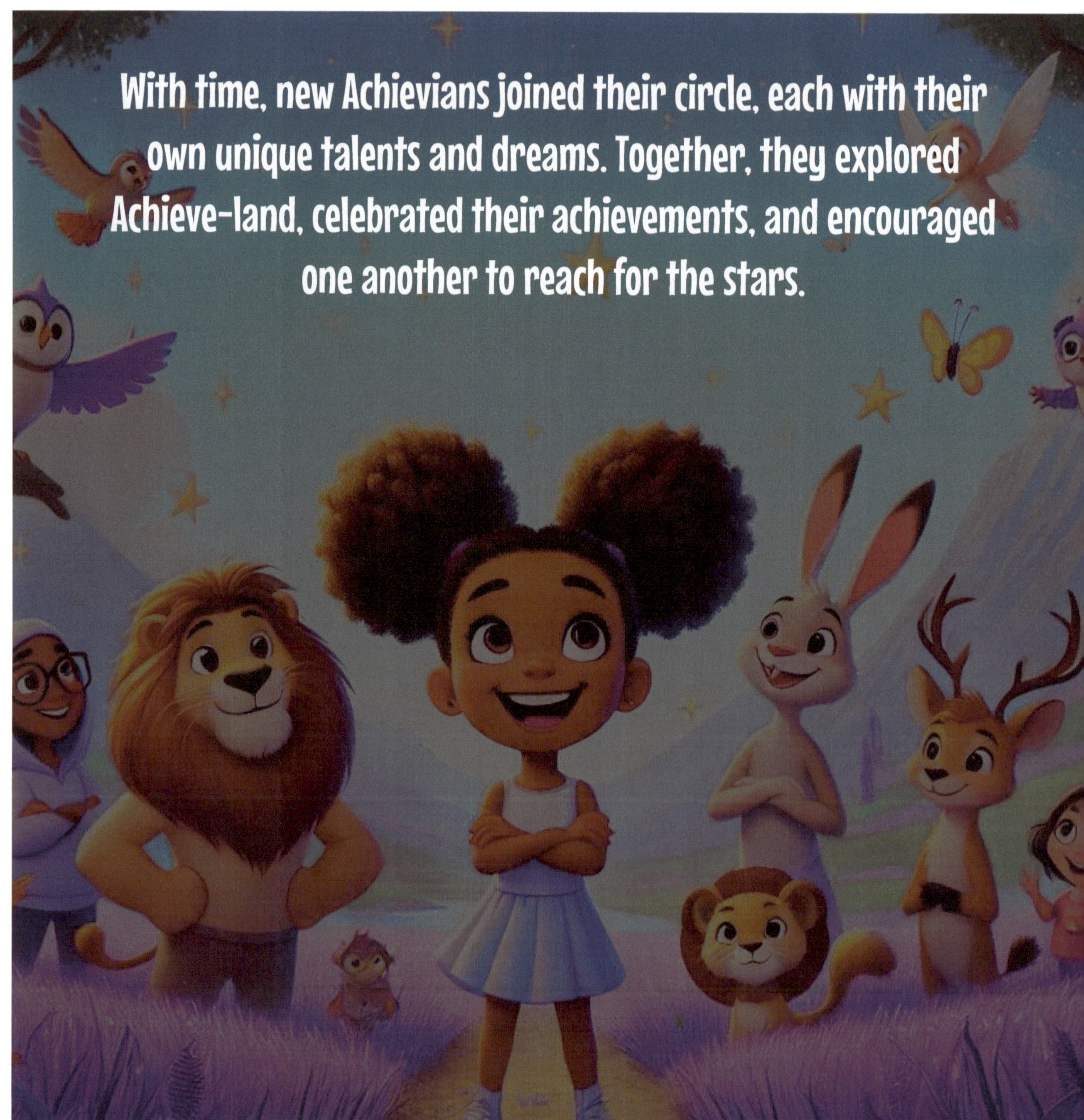

With time, new Achievians joined their circle, each with their
own unique talents and dreams. Together, they explored
Achieve-land, celebrated their achievements, and encouraged
one another to reach for the stars.

As years passed, Alexis' dream of becoming a marine biologist was realized. The flag they planted in Achieve-land was replaced with real diving gear and a research vessel, symbols of her success and unwavering belief in herself.

The magic of Achieve-land lives within us all, waiting to inspire and guide us on our journey to success. As Alexis continued her adventures, she realized that Achieve-land was not just a place but a state of mind, a realm where dreams were born, nurtured, and realized. With the Achieve-land mindset, she could overcome any challenge, achieve any dream, and make the impossible possible.

And so, in Alexis' heart and mind, Achieve-land lived on, a place of infinite possibilities and a reminder that, with determination and self-belief, she could achieve anything she set her mind to.

Join Alexis on a magical journey to Achieve-land, a place where dreams come alive and anything is possible. In this enchanting tale, Alexis meets extraordinary friends who inspire her to believe in herself and overcome life's challenges. Dive into this whimsical world and discover the Achievian spirit within you!

In a land where dreams take flight,
And stars twinkle bright each night,
Lives a spark in every heart,
A special magic, a wondrous art.

Alexis found this place of cheer,
Where Achievians hold dreams dear,
From Sparkle's glow to Roxy's leap,
Each tale of courage she did keep.

With each story, a lesson learned,
A flame of hope inside her burned,
Through mazes, rivers, forests deep,
Her heart stayed strong, her spirit leap.

Believe in yourself, let courage rise,
With every challenge, you grow wise,
In Achieve-land or real life's strand,
You hold the magic, take your stand.

Embrace your dreams with all your might,
For you are the light that shines so bright.